Timothy and Sarah
The Homemade Cake Contest

Story and Pictures by Midori Basho

Timothy & Sarah

Little twin mice, Timothy and Sarah,
were looking out the window.
They saw Miss Flora, who lived nearby,
coming their way.
They ran to the door to greet her.

"Hello, Timothy," said Miss Flora.
"Hello, Sarah."
"Hello, Miss Flora," said the
little mice.
"Is your mother at home?"
asked Miss Flora.

2

Miss Flora followed the twins into the house. As she was taking off her jacket, she said, "Mother, I have come today to ask you something."

"Oh, really," said Mother. "Please have a seat. I was just about to make some tea."

Sarah and Timothy joined Mother and Miss Flora at the table.

"Well, do you know of the house on the outskirts of our town that has stood empty for quite a long time?" Miss Flora asked Mother.

"Ah, you mean that old house that has been abandoned," said Mother.

"Do you mean the haunted house?" asked the twins.

"Oh, yes, children call it the haunted house, don't they?" said Miss Flora.

"But you know," she continued, "it was once a very nice place. In fact, it was a little café that stood in what was then the forest. I would stop there with my children when we went for walks. We could smell the freshly baked bread."

"We grown-ups could talk together while we drank our tea," said Miss Flora. "The children would play nearby in the forest. We all had a wonderful time."

As Miss Flora talked, she looked fondly into the distance.

"Time passed and the café closed. The house was abandoned and became rundown before we knew it," Miss Flora sighed sadly.

"Every time I pass by that house, I feel sad remembering how it used to be," said Miss Flora, looking in Mother's eyes. "I think we should do something about the house."

Then Miss Flora explained her plan. "I would like to repair the house and bring it back again. I want to make it an oasis where elderly people and children can all get together and have fun."

"What a wonderful idea," said Mother. "We should all work together to

make it happen."

"But, we would have to buy materials to fix the house," said Miss Flora.

Her face suddenly had a worried look. "And that might cost a lot of money."

"Maybe we could collect money from the people of the town?" said Mother. The two

ladies started thinking seriously about how

they might do this.

While all this was going on, Timothy and Sarah

were munching on cake as a snack.

So, Miss Flora took a bite of the cake, too.

"Wow, it's delicious!" she exclaimed.

"Thank you," Mother said, "I baked it just

this morning."

"That's wonderful. How did you make this?" Miss

Flora said.

Suddenly the fork in her hand stopped in midair. "Oh,

my, I just had an idea."

"Why don't we bake cakes and sell them to people?" she said. "That would be a way to raise the money."

"That's a wonderful idea," said Mother. "But… I'm afraid we may not earn enough to repair the house." Then, her face suddenly brightened and she looked at Miss Flora.

"I have an idea," said Mother. What if we asked people to bring in their own homemade cakes? We would have many more cakes this way. And everyone could vote to choose the best cake. Then, we could sell all the cakes."

"That's a great idea!" exclaimed Miss Flora. "A homemade cake contest!"

"I am sure it's going to be a big success," said Mother. And she and Miss Flora continued talking about the cake contest until dusk.

So, they decided to have a homemade cake contest.

Miss Flora and Mother made posters announcing the contest. They put up the posters at many places around the town.

They told their friends about the homemade cake contest and also asked them to tell their friends.

Timothy and Sarah decided to make their own cakes and enter them in the contest.

They looked at books with pictures of cakes. They drew their own pictures of cakes. They were trying to decide what kind of cake to make.

Finally, the twins were ready to start. That's when they realized that they were not sure how to make cake dough. So Mother taught them and helped them make the dough.

With his strong arms, Father helped, too, by whisking the cream and egg whites.

Timothy decided to bake a cake that would have
lots of walnuts. These are his favorite kind of nut.
First, he baked the cake with walnuts inside. Then,
he decorated the cake with more walnuts and some
different kinds of nuts.

Then Timothy drew his face on the cake. Finally he
put the cake back in the oven for a short time to
finish it. The aroma was fantastic.

Sarah also decided to bake a cake that she would love
to eat. It was a strawberry shortcake.
Unfortunately, the first sponge cake she baked came
out flat. It did not rise.
She tried again. Her second cake came out nice and
fluffy.
She put on a lot of creamy icing. To finish her cake, she
decorated it with strawberries, blueberries and mint.
Her cake was very colorful.

Mother made a chocolate cake. She placed a stencil, a piece of paper with cutout figures, on top and sprinkled powdered sugar over it.

Then she counted one, two, three and lifted up the paper. The silhouettes of two angels appeared on the cake.

Father had another job to do. He made medals for the winners of the contest. He made a gold medal, a silver medal and a bronze medal, by cutting them out of cardboard.

"I wonder who will win these medals?" asked Mother.

"I want the gold medal," said Timothy.

"I want it, too," said Sarah.

The contest was to begin soon.

The homemade cake contest was held at the park in town. Timothy and Sarah arrived with Mother and Father, carrying their special cakes.

A large tent had been set up. Lots of contestants and other visitors had already gathered.

There were so many cakes on the tables!

"Look, it's Miss Flora!" said Sarah.

Timothy and Sarah rushed over to her. Miss Flora's cake had lots of flowers on it and looked very beautiful.

"Wow, your cake is so nice!" said Timothy.

"Thank you," Miss Flora said with shining eyes. "Look at everyone's cakes. They are all wonderful!"

As Miss Flora had said, the tables were crowded with many kinds of cakes. Timothy and Sarah found their friends' cakes.

Millie's cake had a ballerina made of marzipan dancing on it.

Susan's cake was an apple pie. It was slightly burnt here and there.

All the cakes were on display.

There was a rose cake, an acorn cake, a steam engine cake, and a little bird cake. Ah, there was also a worm cake. All the cakes were different, but they all looked very tasty.

"Attention everyone, the judges are about to begin," said the mailman loudly. He was the chief judge.

First, the judges looked for cakes that were beautiful or fun.

All the people watched quietly.

Then, the judges tasted the cakes.

"This cake is almost too beautiful to cut," said the
mailman, putting a knife in the cake.
The judges ate a small piece of each cake.

"Wow!" said one judge.
"Well, well," said another.

Watching them tasting all
those cakes, Timothy and
Sarah's mouths watered.

Finally, the judges huddled together whispering
about the cakes.

"Well, we are about to announce the results!" proclaimed the mailman.

At just that moment, a little mouse named Rick came running into the tent. He was huffing and puffing and carrying a big box.

"Wait, wait! May I please enter the contest?"

"I'm sorry for getting here late," said Rick, "but I just finished my cake. Am I too late?"

"No, not at all," said the mailman. "We welcome everyone!" And everyone was happy to have Rick join the cake contest.

"I'm glad. Thank you." Rick happily opened his box.

Then what he lifted from the box was this!

It was a wonderful candy house! Not only the house but all the flowers and trees around it were made of candy. There were toys and a table and chairs in the yard. All made of candy. There were children playing and grandpa and grandma. Everything was made with candy. What a fun-looking cake it was.

"Wow!" Everyone gasped at the same time.

"Well, now we are going to present the winners," the mailman shouted so everyone in the noisy crowd could hear.

The bronze medal for third place went to a banana cake covered with fruit.

The silver medal for second place was given to Miss Flora's flower cake.

And the first prize went to…
"We the judges unanimously present the gold medal to Rick's candy house," the mailman said.

"As soon as we saw the candy house, our minds were decided. Apologies to the other contestants."

Loud applause came from all the people.

"Thank you for waiting," said the mailman. "Now, please buy pieces of the cakes you like."

A box was placed in front of each cake. The guests set the price themselves for the cakes that they liked, and put the money into the boxes.

Timothy and Sarah were a little disappointed that they did not receive the gold medal, but they were more interested now in having a taste of the cakes just as soon as they could.

"Which cake should I taste first?" asked Timothy.

"Are they going to buy a piece of my cake?" said Sarah.

Timothy's walnut cake, Sarah's strawberry shortcake, and Mother's chocolate cake were all sold out in the blink of an eye.

Miss Flora bought Susan's apple pie.

However, no one had tasted Rick's first-prize candy house.

They could not cut the candy house into pieces as they could the cakes. Should they break it apart and sell the pieces?

Everyone was wondering what to do.

Then, an old gentleman came forward. He bought the candy house at a surprisingly high price.

The gentleman explained that his wife was sick. "My wife looks sad every day. But I believe she is going to get her smile back when she sees this candy cake. You see, it looks just like the house we used to live in."

Rick put his candy house in the box and gave it to him, saying, "Thank you very much, sir. I hope your wife will feel better."

After that, everyone either sat around the park and ate their cakes or took their pieces of cake home.

Besides the cakes, the cakes' recipes, cookies, and bread were also sold. As a result, a lot of money was raised at the cake contest.

The money from the cake contest enabled Miss Flora and Mother to buy materials to repair the old, abandoned house.

Many people who were good at carpentry came to help.

Other people helped in different ways.

Timothy, Sarah and other children also helped.

One of the carpenters told Miss Flora that he had played around the house when he was child. "I was very sad to see this house standing empty for so long. I am very happy that I can help today."

Then, a lady who was handing out sandwiches to people for lunch said, "I have always told my children that this was not a haunted house at all. It had once been a very nice place. Thank you, Miss Flora, for thinking of such a good idea."

As they worked on the old house, everyone began thinking of the "candy house" that Rick had made.

"Let's make it like that house!" Everyone agreed. And they repeated this to one another the whole time that they worked on the house. It became a slogan for their work.

And in the end, the old house stood revived all new like a wonder.

Then, Rick built benches and placed them here and there.

The carpenters used leftover materials to build a set of swings in the yard.

"Yahoo!" Everyone cheered. "Fantastic!"

Timothy and Sarah also cheered at the beautiful house.

They cleaned out the once-ruined garden. They planted many flowers and made a small pond as well.

Then, they planted some trees that would grow fruit around the house.

"When these trees grow and bear their delicious fruit," said Miss Flora, "this house will once again be the source of many new and happy memories for people."

The house was finally completed.

A housewarming party was planned for
the next day.

When the next day came, many elderly people and children gathered. They all made themselves at home as they liked.

Ah! The old gentleman

is coming, too...

And, the door of this house is always open.

Timothy and Sarah:
The Homemade Cake Contest

Translation by Mariko Shii Gharbi
English editing by Richard Stull

Published in the United States by:
Museyon Inc.
2 W. 46th St., Mezz. 209
New York, NY 10036

Museyon is a registered trademark.
Visit us online at www.museyon.com

Originally published in Japan in 2010 by Poplar Publishing Co., Ltd.
English translation rights arranged with Poplar Publishing Co., Ltd.

Manufactured by: Regent Publishing Service Ltd., Hong Kong
Printed in Shenzhen, Guangdong, China

ISBN 978-1-940842-02-8

1458080